For the baby

PUFFIN BOOKS

Published by the Penguin Group: London, New York, Australia, Canada, India, Ireland, New Zealand and South Africa
Penguin Books Ltd, Registered Offices: 80 Strand, London WC2R 0RL, England

puffinbooks.com

First published by Viking 1981
Published in Puffin Books 1983
Published in this edition 2011

001 – 10 9 8 7 6 5 4 3 2 1

Made and printed in China

ISBN: 978–0–141–33710–4

PEEPO!

by

Janet & Allan Ahlberg

PUFFIN BOOKS

Here's a little baby
One, two, three
Stands in his cot
What does he see?

PEEPO!

He sees his father sleeping
In the big brass bed
And his mother too
With a hairnet on her head.

He sees the shadows moving
On the bedroom wall
And the sun at the window
And his teddy
And his ball.

Here's a little baby
One, two, three
Sits in his high chair
What does he see?

PEEPO!

He sees his mother pouring
Hot porridge in a bowl
And his father in the doorway
With a bucketful of coal.

He sees his sisters skipping
In the yard outside
And his grandma pegging washing
On the clothes-line
To be dried.

Here's a little baby
One, two, three
Sits in his pushchair
What does he see?

PEEPO!

He sees a bonfire smoking
  Pigeons in the sky
His mother cleaning windows
  A dog going by.

He sees his sisters searching
  For a jar or tin
To take up to the park
  And catch fishes in.

Here's a little baby
One, two, three
Sits on the grass
What does he see?

PEEPO!

He sees his sisters fishing
  With a brown stocking net
And dresses tucked in knickers
  And legs shiny wet.

He sees the tassels blowing
  On his grandma's shawl
And the fringe on the pushchair
  And his teddy
  And his ball.

Here's a little baby
One, two, three
Sits on his sister's lap
What does he see?

PEEPO!

He sees his grandma ironing
His father pouring tea
His other sister squabbling
She wants him on *her* knee.

He sees his mother dozing
In the easy chair
And a dog in the doorway
Who shouldn't be there.

Here's a little baby
One, two, three
Sits in his bath-tub
What does he see?

PEEPO!

He sees his father kneeling
  With his sleeves rolled up
And the flannel on the table
  And the soap
  In a cup.

He sees his nightie warming
  On the oven door
His sisters in the clothes-horse
  Puddles on the floor.

Here's a little baby
One, two, three
On his way to bed
What does he see?

PEEPO!

He sees the landing mirror
   With its rainbow rim
And a mother with a baby
   Just like him.

He sees the bedroom door
   The cot made ready
His father kissing him goodnight
   His ball
   And his teddy.

Here's a little baby
One, two, three
Fast asleep and dreaming
What did he see?

THE END